THIS BOOK BELONGS TO

_____

For Mum, Dad, Frances and Fergal – WH

Special thanks to Emilie and Augusta – LDB

Published by Little Door Books 2019

This edition published 2019

ISBN: 978-0-9927520-9-5

A CIP catalogue record for this book is available from the British Library.

Little Door Books and Little Door Debuts acknowledges support from the National Lottery through Creative Scotland towards the publication of this title.

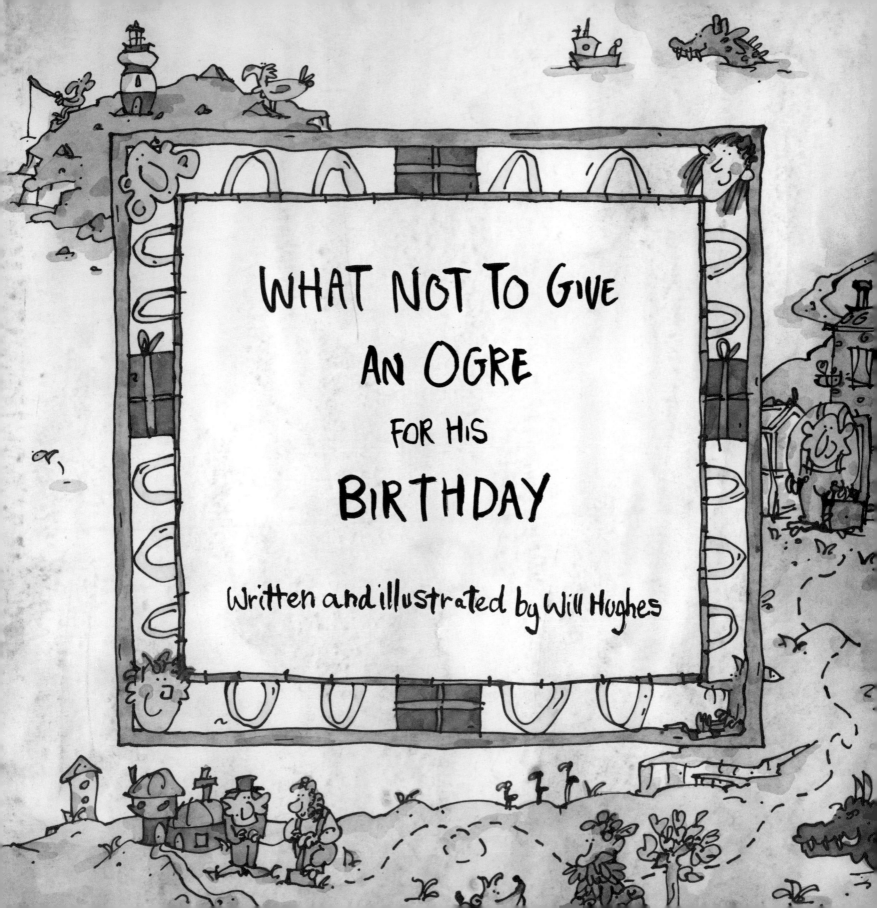

WHAT NOT TO GIVE AN OGRE FOR HIS BIRTHDAY

Written and illustrated by Will Hughes

Stanley and Martha loved buying birthday presents.

They could always find the right gift.

There was only one exception...

...a rather large ogre called Len who had just moved in next door.

All of his friends lived far away, so Stanley and Martha wanted to get Len something special.

But what DO you get an ogre for his birthday?

You could get him a bike...

...but that might be a bad idea.

You could get him an exciting shirt...

...or a pair of colourful socks.

Maybe not.

You could take him to see a play at the theatre, but everyone else might think that was a REALLY bad idea.

And there are lots of reasons why a pet might be a problem.

You could take him on a balloon trip...

...hmmm, that might not work

You could take him to visit a castle...

REALLY HEAVY OWL

...although that might end
in disaster.

And a trip to the museum could get you into a lot of trouble.

LONG ARMED LARRY
DON'T TOUCH

Or what about taking him to the fanciest restaurant in town?

Well, that could be VERY expensive.

It seemed that there was nothing you could get an ogre for his birthday.

Then Stanley and Martha had a BRILLIANT idea.

They wrote letters to all of Len's friends

inviting them to a party.

His friends said they were on their way.

And
when they
arrived...

...Len had one of the BEST BIRTHDAYS EVER!

THE END

Will Hughes is an illustrator, author and cartoonist from Malvern in Worcestershire. He graduated with a degree in illustration from Edinburgh College of Art in 2017 and has since been working as a freelance illustrator. Whatever he makes, he likes his work to be lively, comic, fun and to tell the stories of all sorts of characters. From an old woman with a hoard of very helpful cats to burglars who have to stand on each others shoulders to rob a house. "What Not To Give An Ogre For His Birthday" is Will's first published children's book but he hopes to make many more.

He is very excited to have been chosen to be part of the 2018/19 Picturehooks picture book mentoring scheme. If you would like any more information about Will's work you can visit www.willustrations.co.uk

Here at Little Door Books, our aim is to find and encourage undiscovered illustration talent and it is our hope that we can help these gifted individuals get the best start on their journey in publishing and that we can inspire them to produce exciting work now and in the future. We are thrilled to be working with Will on his amazing debut picture book, we hope that you love it as much as we do.

Little Door Debuts was set up in 2019 and is dedicated to ensuring everyone knows just how important illustrators are to the success of children's books. If you would like to join us in helping new creatives shine, please go to the website and join our mailing list. www.littledoorbooks.co.uk

A huge THANK YOU to you all ...

ISHBEL MCLACHLAN

BARRY HUTCHISON

JULIE AND ALAN WEST

CAROL McNAUGHTON

GRAHAM AND ANDREA POGSON

CATHERINE THOMANN

TO EMILIE, THANKS FOR
EVERYTHING FROM LDB

JULIE AND ANDREW MENCNAROWSKI

JUERGEN GERBER

LINDSAY LITTLESON

VIVIAN FRENCH

LÉA TIMSIT

TO MIKE, HAPPY 50TH
BIRTHDAY FROM A & S

SARA SHERIDAN

EMMI KOIVISTO

JO WOOLF

KATHERINE SNOW

KIRSTIN LAMB

JO RIGGALL

TO ALAN FROM SUSAN

LOUISA MACDOUGALL

KATIE LLEWELLIN

EMILIE BAGGER

LINDSEY FRASER

SUSAN WINDRAM

TO JACK FROM
GRANDMA AND GRANDAD

TINA EVANS

EMMA PALLEN

ALAN WINDRAM

ANTHEA PITT

STEPHEN DAY

TO MIA FROM DAD

GILLIAN AND DARREN MCKINNON

ALLAN PETTIE

TO ANDREW AND GAVIN FROM MUM AND DAD

LORNA ROSE TREEN

FIONA SCOTT

SARA O'CONNOR

HANNAH FOLEY

TO SUSAN FROM ALAN

PIPPA GOODHART

DAVID AND PAULA OGILVIE

JIM AND MOIRA FISKEN

IAN AND LINDSAY BLAIR

MERRIOL BALDWIN

We couldn't have done it without YOU!